DATE DUE

2-10 N			

HIGHSMITH 45-102   PRINTED IN U.S.A.

WHISTLEforWILLIE

Also by Ezra Jack Keats

THE SNOWY DAY

WHISTLE

FOR WILLIE

New York · The Viking Press

To Ann

Oh, how Peter wished he could whistle!

7

He saw a boy playing with his dog. Whenever the boy whistled, the dog ran straight to him.

Peter tried and tried to whistle, but he couldn't.
So instead he began to turn himself around—
around and around he whirled . . .
faster and faster . . . .

When he stopped
everything turned
down . . .
and up . . .

and up . . .

and down . . .

and around

and around.

Peter saw his dog, Willie, coming.
Quick as a wink, he hid in an empty
carton lying on the sidewalk.

"Wouldn't it be funny if I whistled?" Peter thought.
"Willie would stop and look all around to see
who it was."

Peter tried again to whistle—but still he couldn't.
So Willie just walked on.

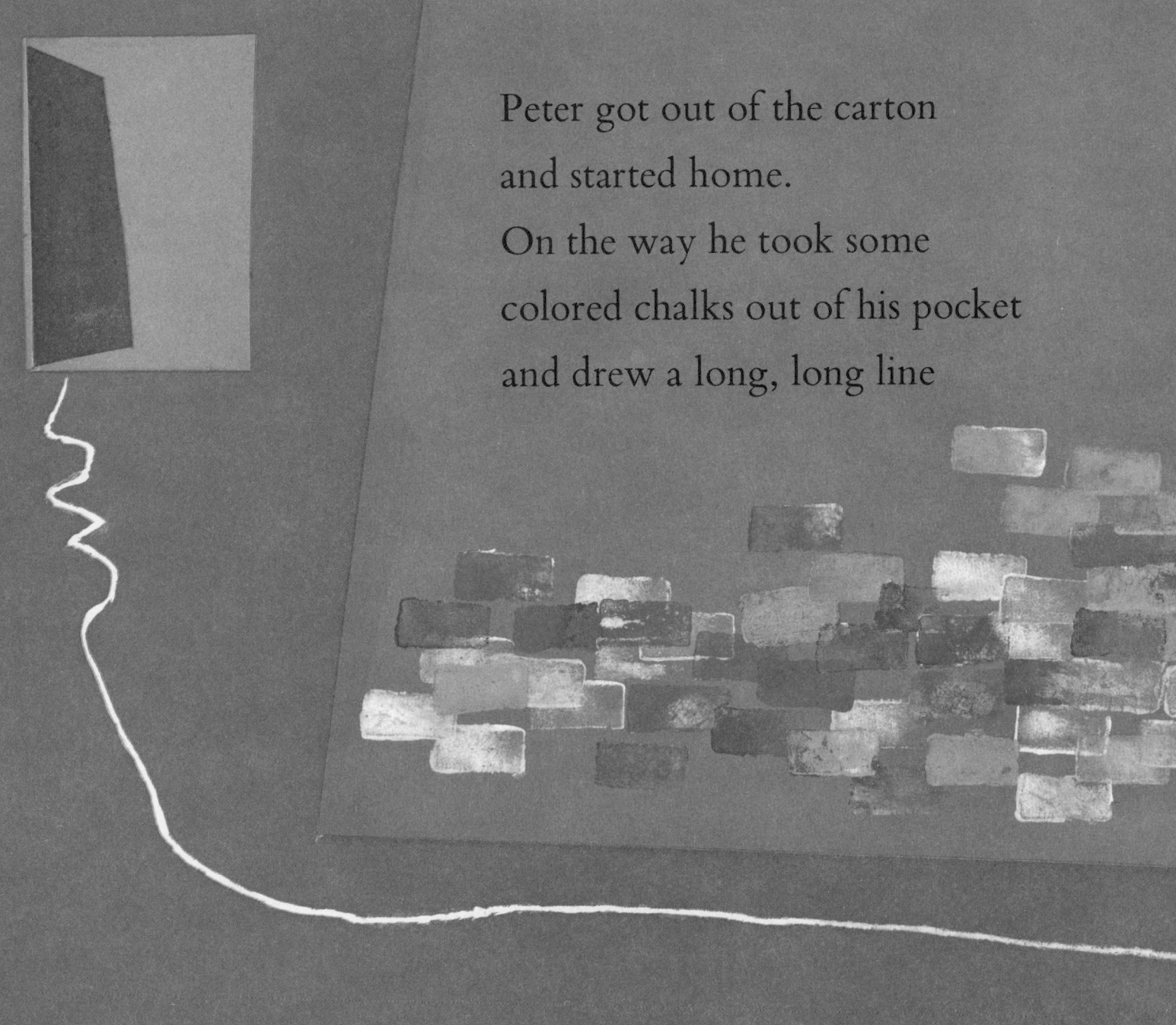

Peter got out of the carton
and started home.
On the way he took some
colored chalks out of his pocket
and drew a long, long line

right up to his door.

He stood there and tried to whistle again.

He blew till his cheeks were tired.

But nothing happened.

18

He went into his house and put on his father's
old hat to make himself feel more grown-up.
He looked into the mirror to practice whistling.
Still no whistle!

When his mother saw what he was doing,
Peter pretended that he was his father.
He said, "I've come home early today, dear. Is Peter here?"

His mother answered,

"Why no, he's outside with Willie."

"Well, I'll go out and look for them," said Peter.

First he walked along a crack in the sidewalk.
Then he tried to run away from his shadow.

He jumped off his shadow.
But when he landed
they were
together
again.

He came to the corner
where the carton was,
and who should he see but Willie!

Peter scrambled under the carton.

He blew and blew and blew.

Suddenly—out came a real whistle!

Willie stopped and looked around to see
who it was.

"It's me," Peter shouted, and stood up.

Willie raced straight to him.

Peter ran home
to show his father and mother what he could do.
They loved Peter's whistling. So did Willie.

Peter's mother asked him and Willie

to go on an errand to the grocery store.

He whistled all the way there,
and he whistled all the way home.